Eight
Animals
on the Town

To the cousins: Jake, Alex, Carolyn,
Katie, Kelsey, Nicholas, Sam,
Josh, Janine, and Torrie
—S.M.E.

To animals everywhere
—L.C.

Eight
Animals
on the Town

Susan Middleton Elya

illustrated by Lee Chapman

G. P. Putnam's Sons

Eight **animales**, ready to eat,
head to the market
on animal feet.

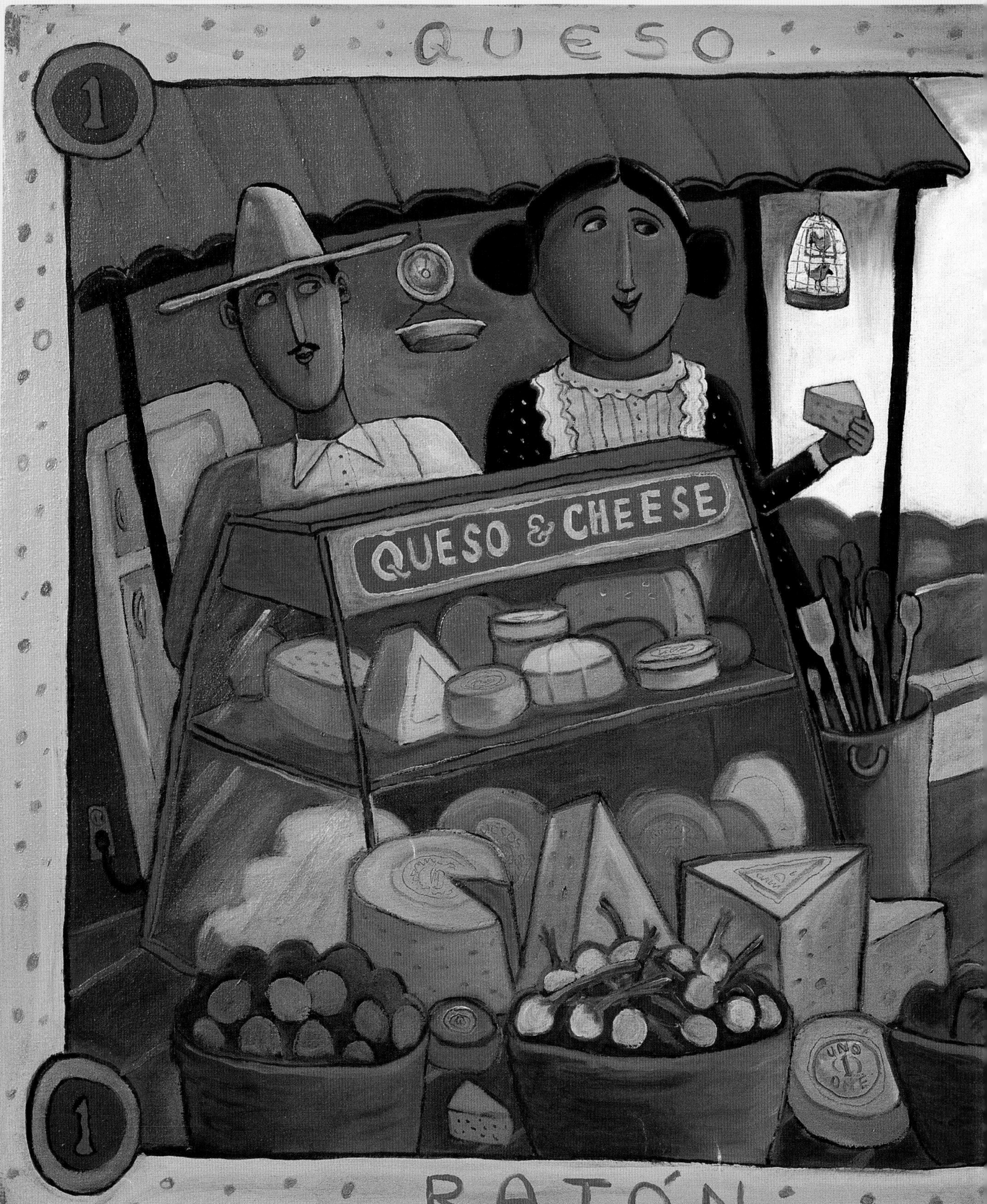
QUESO
1
QUESO & CHEESE
UNO
1
ONE
1
RATÓN

First comes a mouse. He's a **ratón**.
Número uno, out on his own.
Off to the market he hurries for cheese.
"Since I'm a **ratón**, I'd like **queso**, please."

Next comes a cat,
número dos.
Second in line,
getting too close.
Cat wants to buy
a bottle of milk.
"**Leche**,"
purrs **Gato**,
as smoothly
as silk.

BONE = HUESO

Then comes a dog,
número tres.
Third to the market,
his favorite place.
Dog pushes on
to buy a big bone.
"**Un hueso**,"
says **Perro**,
"for my very own."

THREE · DOG = PERRO · TRES

Número cuatro is a large bird.
Fourth in line after first, second, third.
Bird flies along
to purchase some seed.
"**Semillas**," chirps **Pájaro**.
"That's what I need."

Número cinco is a young frog.
Fifth in the line behind Bird and Dog.
Frog hops along, hungry for flies.
"**Moscas**," says **Rana**, "economy size."

Next comes a horse, **número seis**.
Sixth at the market—a big, noisy place.
Horse has decided to purchase some hay.
"**Heno** to go," says **Caballo**.
"Can't stay."

Número siete, a black and white cow,
brings all her milk money saved until now.
She is so hungry, she asks to buy grass.
"Hierba," says **Vaca,**
"and please make it fast."

HENO

HAY
HENO

CABALLO

VACA
7
MORE GRASS
MÁS HIERBA
HIERBA
GRASS
SEVEN
$
SIETE
7
HIERBA

EIGHT PIG=CERDO

Last is the pig, **número ocho.**
He's finally finished his Christmas **bizcocho.**
"I'd like to buy corn because I'm a pig.
A sack of **maíz**," says **Cerdo**, "this big!"

CORN=MAÍZ

Mouse, Cat and Dog are

uno,

dos,

tres,

1

2

3

Bird—**cuatro,**

Frog—**cinco,**

Horse makes it **seis.**

Then Cow and Pig,
the two that
came late,

make **siete**

and **ocho**—

seven and eight.

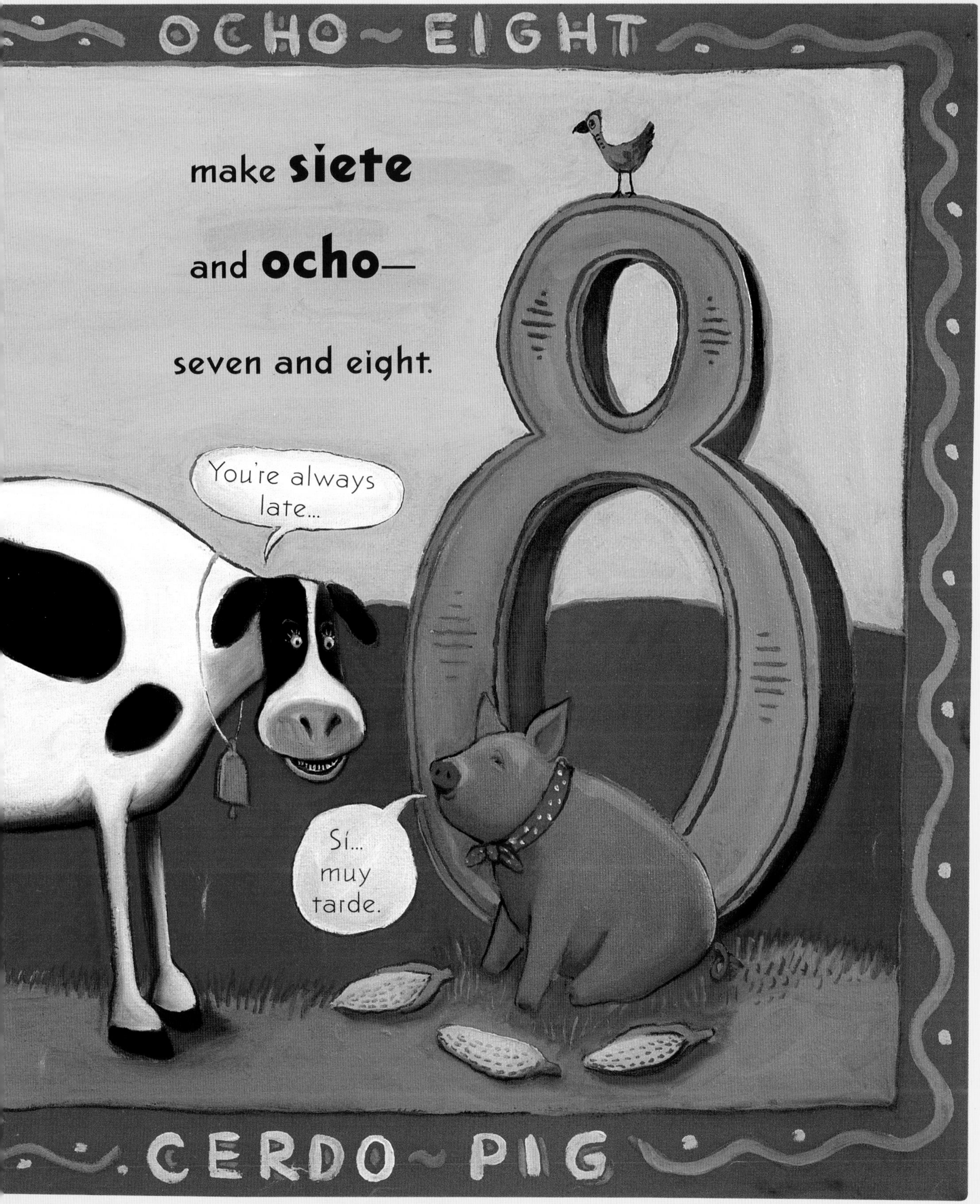

Eight **animales** are in a good mood.
They sit down to supper
and munch on their food.

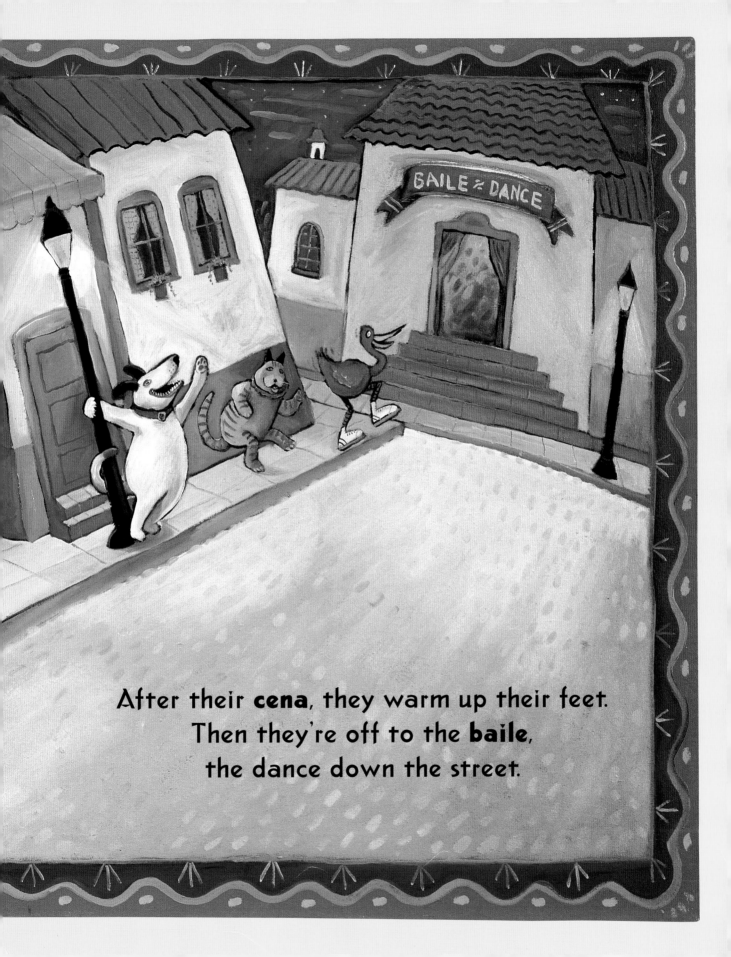

After their **cena**, they warm up their feet.
Then they're off to the **baile**,
the dance down the street.

They dance all night long,

then gather outside,
climb into two cars, and go for a ride.

Eight **animales**,
riding in **coches**,
all say, "Good night."
That's **Buenas noches**.

Glossary and Pronunciation Guide

Abejas (ah BEH hahs) bees

Animales (ah nee MAH lehs) animals

Baile (BYE leh) dance

Bichos finos (BEE choce FEE noce) fine bugs

Bizcocho (beece KOE choe) a Mexican
      sugar cookie flavored with anise

Buenas noches (BWEH nahss NOE chehs)
      good night

Caballo (kah BAH yoe) horse

Carnes (KAHR nehs) meats

Cena (SEH nah) supper

Cerdo (SEHR doe) pig

Cinco (SEEN koe) five

Coches (KOE chehs) cars

Cuatro (KWAH troe) four

Cucarachas (koo kah RAH chahs) cockroaches

Dos (DOHS) two

Gato (GAH toe) cat

Gusanos (goo SAH noce) worms

Heno (EH noe) hay

Hierba (YEHR bah) grass

Hormigas (ohr MEE gahs) ants

Hueso (WEH soe) bone

Leche (LEH cheh) milk

Maíz (mah EECE) corn

Más (MAHS) more

Mercado (mehr KAH doe) market

Moscas (MOCE kahs) flies

Muy (MWEE) very

Número (NOO meh roe) number

Ocho (OH choe) eight

Pájaro (PAH hah roe) bird

Perro (PEH rroe) dog

Queso (KEH soe) cheese

Rana (RRAH nah) frog

Ratón (rrah TONE) mouse

Seis (SEHS) six

Semillas (seh MEE yahs) seeds

Sí (SEE) yes

Siete (SYEH teh) seven

Tarde (TAHR deh) late

Tres (TREHS) three

Un (OON) a, an

Uno (OO noe) one

Vaca (VAH kah) cow

Text copyright © 2000 by Susan Middleton Elya
Illustrations copyright © 2000 by Lee Chapman
All rights reserved. This book, or parts thereof, may not be reproduced in any form
without permission in writing from the publisher.
G. P. PUTNAM'S SONS
a division of Penguin Putnam Books for Young Readers,
345 Hudson Street, New York, NY 10014. G. P. Putnam's Sons,
Reg. U.S. Pat. & Tm. Off. Published simultaneously in Canada.
Manufactured in China by South China Printing Co. Ltd.
Designed by Semadar Megged.
The art for this book was created using oil paints on canvas.
Library of Congress Cataloging-in-Publication Data
Elya, Susan Middleton, 1955-
Eight animals on the town / by Susan Middleton Elya ; illustrated by Lee Chapman. p. cm.
Summary: Eight animals go to market, to supper, and to dance, introducing the numbers
from one to eight and vocabulary in English and Spanish.
ISBN 0-399-23437-3
[1. Animals—Fiction. 2. Counting. 3. Spanish language—Vocabulary. 4. Stories in rhyme.]
I. Chapman, Lee, ill. II. Title. PZ8.3.E514 Ei 2000 [E]—dc21 99-055269
3 5 7 9 10 8 6 4